With special thanks to the SpongeBob SquarePants writers

Based on the TV series *SpongeBob SquarePants®*
created by Stephen Hillenburg as seen on Nickelodeon®

SIMON SPOTLIGHT
An imprint of Simon & Schuster Children's Publishing Division
1230 Avenue of the Americas, New York, New York 10020

Manufactured in the United States of America

First Edition
2 4 6 8 10 9 7 5 3 1

ISBN 0-689-85072-7

Life's a Beach

and Other SpongeBob-isms

Simon Spotlight/Nickelodeon

New York London Toronto Sydney Singapore

Ahoy there, mates!
Ready to sing the
SpongeBob SquarePants
theme song?

I can't hear you!

OOOOOOOOOOOOHHH,

Who lives in a pineapple under the sea?

SPONGEBOB SQUAREPANTS!

Absorbent and YELLOW and POROUS is he.

SPONGEBOB SQUAREPANTS!

If nautical nonsense be something you wish,

SPONGEBOB SQUAREPANTS!

Then drop on the deck and flop like a fish!

SPONGEBOB SQUAREPANTS!

SPONGEBOB SQUAREPANTS!

SPONGEBOB SQUAREPANTS!

SPONGEBOB SQUAREPANTS!

SPONGE- BOB, SQUARE- PANTS!

Plenty of Fish in the Sea

SpongeBob on Relationships

This isn't just any ordinary ol' handshake! This is a *Friendly* handshake!
Winding up with no one
Is a lot less Fun
Than a burn From the sun
Or sand in your buns.

Mollusks are People Too!

SpongeBob on Snail Care

You know what
they say, Gary,
"Curiosity salted the snail
Mind your wandering eye
you little mollusk.

You need to take Gary on a walk twice a day. His leash is in the closet. In the morning you've got to wax his shell and massage his eyes.

At least I'm safe inside my mind.

IF I close my eyes, it doesn't seem so dark.

SpongeBob ScaredyPants

SpongeBob on Fear

PATRICK: Sometimes we have to go deep inside ourselves to solve our problems.

SPONGEBOB: I'm scared.

PATRICK: Then I'm going in . . . For you!

Oh, Barnacles!

SpongeBob on Failure

PATRICK: Where are we, SpongeBob?

SPONGEBOB: Rock Bottom.

PATRICK: What's that smell?

SPONGEBOB: That, Patrick, is th

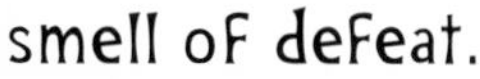

smell of defeat.

Help!
I'm hooked!
There is no Plan B!
No Plan B!

Look at me . . . I’m naked!

SpongeBob on Vanity

SpongeBob FryCook

SpongeBob on Career

This is more fun than double overtime at the Krusty Krab!

Time to get some rest. I don't want to look tired for my Employee-of-the-Month photo.

The perfect patties are made with love, not magic.

A Friend in Seaweed Is a Friend Indeed

SpongeBob on Friendship

No, you can't pop him! He's not just a bubble! He's a bubble buddy! He's my friend, and I love him!

As long as these pants are square
and this sponge is BOB,
I will not let you down!

Unsinkable!
SpongeBob on Self-Esteem
I am confident in my abilities to successfully succeed.

Now, I learned a lesson
I won't soon forget.
So listen up and
you won't regret.
Be true to yourself,
don't miss your chance,
And you won't
end up like the fool who
ripped his pants!

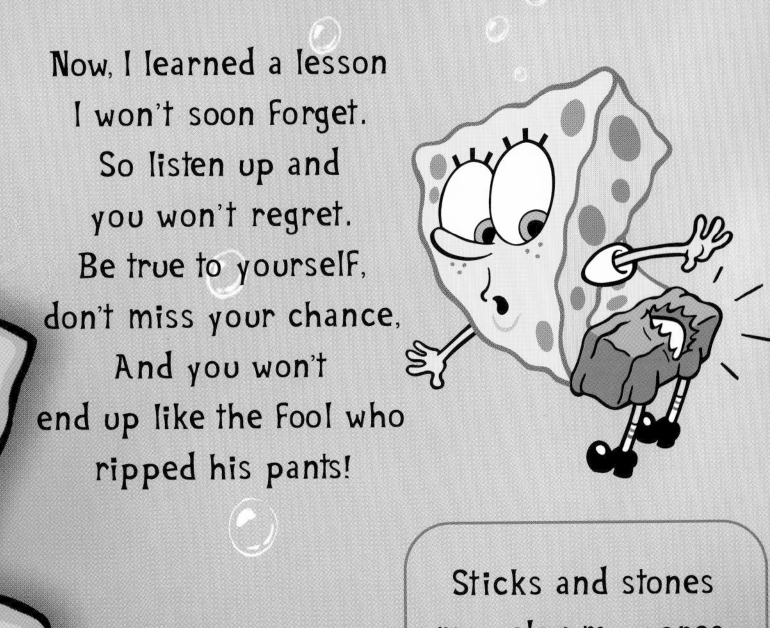

MuscleBob BuffPants

SpongeBob on Fitness

A sponge has got
to look his spongiest.

The Art of Being SpongeBob

SpongeBob on Motivation

Don't give up, Patrick! This time I've got something I know you can do! We're going to . . . open a jar!

Don't be a stick in the sand.

Nautical Nonsense

SpongeBob on Life in Bikini Bottom

Oh, tartar sauce!
I'm going to a
different dream.

This really IS
your best day ever.

C'mon, crack of dawn! Start cracking!
Did I do something funny?